Philippines

STEVE GOLDSWORTHY

www.av2books.com

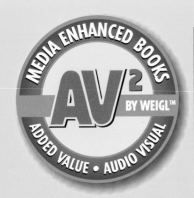

AV² provides enriched content that supplements and complements this book. Weigl's AV² books strive to create inspired learning and engage young minds in a total learning experience.

Your AV² Media Enhanced books come alive with...

Audio
Listen to sections of the book read aloud.

Key Words
Study vocabulary, and complete a matching word activity.

Video
Watch informative video clips.

Quizzes
Test your knowledge.

Embedded Weblinks
Gain additional information for research.

Slide Show
View images and captions, and prepare a presentation.

Try This!
Complete activities and hands-on experiments.

... and much, much more!

Go to **www.av2books.com**, and enter this book's unique code.

BOOK CODE

H664586

AV² by Weigl brings you media enhanced books that support active learning.

Published by AV² by Weigl
350 5th Avenue, 59th Floor
New York, NY 10118
Websites: www.av2books.com   www.weigl.com

Library of Congress Cataloging-in-Publication Data

Goldsworthy, Steve.
 Philippines / Steve Goldsworthy.
   pages cm. — (Exploring countries)
 Includes index.
 ISBN 978-1-4896-3062-9 (hard cover : alk. paper) — ISBN 978-1-4896-3063-6 (soft cover : alk. paper) — ISBN 978-1-4896-3064-3 (single user ebook) — ISBN 978-1-4896-3065-0 (multi-user ebook)
 1. Philippines—Juvenile literature. 2. Philippines—Description and travel—Juvenile literature. I. Title.
 DS655.G64 2014
 959.9—dc23

                              2014038997

Printed in the United States of America in Brainerd, Minnesota
1 2 3 4 5 6 7 8 9 19 18 17 16 15

012015
WEP160115

Project Coordinator Heather Kissock
Art Director Terry Paulhus

Photo Credits
Every reasonable effort has been made to trace ownership and to obtain permission to reprint copyright material. The publishers would be pleased to have any errors or omissions brought to their attention so that they may be corrected in subsequent printings.

Weigl acknowledges Getty Images as its primary image supplier for this title.

Contents

Philippines Overview

The Philippines is an island nation. It is located on the western edge of the Pacific Ocean in Southeast Asia. The country features mountain ranges, fertile valleys, and a beautiful coastline. The Philippines was once ruled by Spain. It later became a United States **commonwealth**. The country gained its independence in 1946. Since then, the **Republic** of the Philippines has been its official name.

People of the Philippines are called Filipinos.

The Tubbataha Reefs in the Sulu Sea are home to many colorful plants and animals.

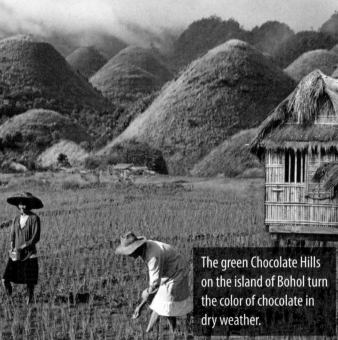

The green Chocolate Hills on the island of Bohol turn the color of chocolate in dry weather.

Philippine tarsiers are native to the southeast. Adults weigh less than half a pound (225 grams).

Paoay Church in the northern Philippines was built in 1710. It features a coral stone bell tower and supports called buttresses for protection from earthquakes.

Exploring the Philippines

The Philippines covers a total area of 115,830 square miles (300,000 square kilometers). It is made up of 7,107 islands. Nine of its islands make up 90 percent of the land. They include Luzon, Mindanao, Palawan, Panay, and Mindoro. The Philippines is north of parts of Malaysia and Indonesia. It is south of Taiwan, southeast of China, and east of Vietnam. Several bodies of water that connect to the Pacific Ocean surround the Philippines. The Philippine Sea is to the east. The Celebes Sea is to the south, and the Sulu Sea is to the southwest. The South China Sea lies to the west, and the Luzon Strait is to the north.

China

Vietnam

Cagayan River

N

Manila

Map Legend

 Philippines

 Cagayan River

Capital City

 Land

▲ Mount Apo

SCALE | 75 Miles | 75 Kilometers

Water

Taal Lake

Cagayan River

Stretching for 220 miles (350 km), the Cagayan River is the longest river in the Philippines. It begins in the Sierra Madre mountain range of northeastern Luzon. The river flows north through agricultural plains and empties into the Luzon Strait.

Luzon Strait

South China Sea

Sulu Sea

Philippine Sea

Malaysia

Manila

Taal Lake

Mount Apo

Manila

Manila is the capital city of the Philippines. It is located on Manila Bay in southeastern Luzon. Manila is one of the Philippines' busiest ports.

Taal Lake

Taal Lake on Luzon is one of the largest lakes in the Philippines. It covers 94 square miles (244 sq. km) and surrounds Volcano Island. The lake is part of the Taal Volcano National Park, established in 1967.

Mount Apo

Mount Apo, on the island of Mindanao, is the highest peak in the Philippines. It measures 9,692 feet (2,954 meters) high. Mount Apo is an active volcano in the Cordillera Central mountain range. "Active" means that the volcano has erupted within the past 10,000 years.

LAND AND CLIMATE

The Philippine **archipelago** is shaped like a triangle. The Luzon island group is in the north and west. The Visayan islands are in the center. The Mindanao island group is in the south. The land of the Philippines is mostly mountains with coastal lowlands.

The longest mountain range in the Philippines is the Sierra Madre. It stretches north–south along the northern half of the east coast of Luzon. The Cordillera Central also runs north–south through Luzon. Between these two ranges is the Cagayan Valley, which is known for its rich soil. Along the northwest coast of Luzon is the Iloco range. The Diuata Mountains are near the eastern coast of Mindanao.

After the Mount Pinatubo volcano erupted in 1991, ash covered nearby areas.

The Philippines has more than 50 volcanoes. It is part of the Ring of Fire, an area around the edges of the Pacific Ocean that contains more volcanoes than any other region of Earth. Mount Pinatubo on Luzon erupted in 1991, for the first time in more than 500 years. The gases that were released into the air spread around the world. These gases blocked some sunlight, causing a drop in temperatures worldwide of about 1° Fahrenheit (0.5° Celsius) until 1993.

Many rivers cross the islands of the Philippines. The Agno and Pampanga Rivers flow through the central plain of Luzon. The Pasig River flows through the city of Manila to Manila Bay. Both the Mindano and Agusan Rivers are found in the fertile valleys of Mindanao. An underground river runs beneath Puerto-Princesa Subterranean River National Park on the island of Palawan.

The Philippines has a tropical climate. Temperatures are warm year-round, and rainfall is plentiful. The islands are hit by typhoons, the name for hurricanes that occur in the western Pacific Ocean. Many parts of the Philippines also experience **monsoons**.

Land and Climate BY THE NUMBERS

350
Number of Philippine islands that are larger than 1 square mile. (2.6 sq. km)

2013 Year that the massive Typhoon Haiyan hit the central Philippines, killing more than 6,000 people.

108.7°F Hottest temperature ever recorded in the Philippines, on May 31, 2014. (42.6°C)

The island of Boracay in the Visayan group has a long white-sand beach and average temperatures of about 88°F (30°C), making it popular with visitors to the Philippines.

PLANTS AND ANIMALS

The Philippines is one of the most biodiverse places on Earth. This means it has a wide variety of plant and animal **species**. Pine trees grow in the forests of Luzon, and lauan trees can be found in the mountainous regions. Large mangrove trees grow in coastal areas. Orchids and other tropical plants bloom on all of the islands.

One of the largest animals found in the Philippines is the water buffalo. A small water buffalo called the tamarau lives on Mindoro. Other animals that live only in the Philippines include Philippine warty pigs, Visayan spotted deer, and Palawan bearcats. The country is home to the world's largest bat, the golden-capped fruit bat.

Thousands of fish species swim in the waters of the Philippines. Crocodiles and green sea turtles live along the coasts of dozens of islands, including near popular beaches. Laws protect these animals from being hunted or harmed.

21,000
Number of known insect species in the Philippines.

Almost 7 Feet
Wingspan of the rare Philippine eagle. (2 m)

2014
Year the Mount Hamiguitan Range Wildlife Sanctuary was named a **UNESCO** World Heritage site.

Green sea turtles can weigh as much as 700 pounds (300 kilograms). They are among the world's largest sea turtles.

NATURAL RESOURCES

The Philippines is rich in natural resources. The country's resources include timber, salt, cobalt, and petroleum, or oil. The Philippines also mines nickel, copper, silver, and gold.

The country's land is a valuable natural resource. The black soils on Luzon and Mindoro are excellent for growing rice. The soils of mountainous regions, which often contain volcanic ash, support fruit trees. Vegetables and other crops thrive in the sandy soils of the coastal regions.

The Philippines produces more than 67 billion kilowatt hours of electricity per year. More than 20 percent comes from hydropower, or electricity produced using the force of moving water. Dams on rivers generate most of the country's hydropower. About 12 percent of electricity comes from other **renewable sources**, such as wind, solar, and geothermal power. Geothermal power, which uses heat that comes to the surface from deep within Earth, is the country's second-largest renewable energy source.

Natural Resources BY THE NUMBERS

138.5 Million Barrels
Size of the Philippines' oil **reserves** of petroleum.

5.5 MILLION TONS
Weight of fish caught every year in the Philippines. (5 million metric tons)

18%
Portion of the land in the Philippines suitable for farming.

Wind turbines, machines that convert the power of the wind into electricity, line the coastal town of Bangui on Luzon.

TOURISM

More than 5 million tourists visited the Philippines in 2013. Most of them were from South Korea, China, Japan, and the United States. The natural beauty of the country's mountains and tropical beaches attracts many visitors. People come to hike, mountain bike, sail, and snorkel.

Three centuries of Spanish rule have influenced the **architecture** and culture of the Philippines. The country offers visitors a number of historical sites. Fort Santiago was built in Manila in 1571. It is the country's oldest Spanish fort.

San Juan, in the northern Philippines, is a popular surfing destination for tourists.

The historic town of Vigan was constructed by the Spanish in the 16th century. It is the best-preserved planned Spanish **colonial** town in Asia. People can ride horse-drawn carriages down cobblestone streets. The Cathedral of St. Paul and the Archbishop's Palace are examples of Spanish architecture in the town.

The main gate of Fort Santiago was rebuilt after being damaged in the 1940s during World War II.

The National Museum of the Philippines was established in 1901. The institution includes the National Art Gallery, the Museum of the Filipino People, and a **planetarium** in Manila. It also operates regional museums in other cities around the country.

More than 22,000 miles (35,000 km) of Philippine coastline provide dozens of beautiful beaches. Sunbathers enjoy the white sands and clear waters of White Beach on Panay in the western part of the Visayan islands. Surfers can ride the waves at Pagudpud at the northern tip of Luzon. Divers and snorkelers can explore the Tubbataha Reefs. **Marine biologists** believe Tubbataha Reefs Natural Park has the greatest diversity of underwater life in the world.

On Luzon, visitors hike or take a boat trip to Pagsanjan, also known as Magdapio, Falls. The falls have a total drop of almost 300 feet (90 m). They are in a lush mountain forest.

Experienced hikers can tackle the towering heights of Mount Dulang-dulang. Located on the island of Mindanao, it is 9,639 feet (2,938 m) tall. This makes it the second-highest mountain in the country.

Most islands have caves that visitors can explore. People often reach cave entrances by boat.

Tourism BY THE NUMBERS

82,000 Acres
Area the Tubbataha Reefs Natural Park covers. (33,200 hectares)

$4 Billion
Amount spent by tourists visiting the Philippines in 2013.

1975 Year that Manila's planetarium opened.

INDUSTRY

The biggest industry in the Philippines is agriculture. Farmers grow corn, bananas, **cassava**, pineapples, and mangoes. They raise animals such as pigs, cows, and chickens. The Philippines is one of the largest producers of rice in the world. It is also a leader in coconut oil and sugar production.

Construction is a major industry in the Philippines. Many types of new structures are needed as the country's population grows. Construction workers build homes and apartment buildings, shopping malls, factories, and office buildings. Construction companies also build roads and bridges for the government.

Manufacturing has become more important to the Philippines' **economy** in recent decades. Major types of goods produced include clothing, processed foods, and electronics items such as televisions. The international electronics firms Intel and Texas Instruments have set up factories in the country. Toyota, Ford, Mitsubishi, and Nissan produce cars in the Philippines, mostly for buyers in the country.

32%
Portion of the **labor force** working in agriculture in the Philippines.

20 Million Tons
Amount of rice produced in the Philippines in 2013. (18 million metric tons)

15% Percentage of workers employed in manufacturing.

In recent years, many workers have found jobs rebuilding homes and roads destroyed by Typhoon Haiyan.

GOODS AND SERVICES

S ervice industries employ more than half of the labor force. People in these industries provide services rather than produce goods. Service workers include doctors, lawyers, teachers, and government employees.

The Philippines has become a leader in providing business services for companies based in other countries. This is called outsourcing. Workers in the Philippines run **call centers**, give technical support for customers, or handle billing needs for companies outside of the country.

The Philippines has many important **trading partners**. More products are exported, or sold, to Japan than to any other country. The United States, China, and Singapore also buy many Philippine goods. The Philippines imports, or brings in, the most goods from the United States, followed by China and Japan. Imported goods include machinery, transportation equipment, **fossil fuels**, iron, and steel.

One of the busiest ports in the Philippines is the Manila International Container Terminal. The terminal is located between Manila's north and south harbors. It handles almost 1 million containers of goods every year.

Goods and Services BY THE NUMBERS

247 Number of airports in the Philippines.

ABOUT 1
Number of doctors for every 1,000 people in the Philippines, less than half the number for the United States.

More Than 1,600
Number of ports in the Philippines.

Restaurant chefs in the Philippines often prepare fresh seafood that has been caught by local fishers.

INDIGENOUS PEOPLES

Scientific evidence suggests people have lived in what is now the Philippines for tens of thousands of years. People called the Negritos arrived in today's Philippines about 30,000 years ago. They came from the islands of Sumatra and Borneo, as well as from Malaya on the mainland. Their descendants live on the Philippine islands of Luzon, Palawan, Negros, and Mindanao. Some early people of the Malayan **ethnic group** came from Taiwan and parts of the present-day countries of Malaysia and Indonesia. Modern-day Philippine cultures such as the Igorots can trace their **ancestors** to these people.

Other groups who arrived brought their social customs. They created settlements called barangays throughout the Philippine islands. Each settlement was led by a datu, or chief, and had nobles. Nobles were people of importance in the community. There were also workers and enslaved people. Early Filipinos knew how to melt iron and made iron tools. They also developed rice fields.

Indigenous Peoples BY THE NUMBERS

70
Number of indigenous groups in the Philippines.

982 AD Year of the first recorded contact between Chinese traders and people of the Philippine islands.

14 TO 17 MILLION
Number of indigenous people in the Philippines today.

During the Imbayah festival, Igorot women parade with baskets of rice to celebrate the harvest.

THE AGE OF EXPLORATION

Arab traders began to arrive from Malaya and Borneo in the early 15ᵗʰ century. They explored the southern areas of Mindanao and ruled over many barangays. The Arabs introduced their religion, Islam. Followers of Islam are called Muslims.

In the 16ᵗʰ century, the Spanish arrived. Portuguese explorer Ferdinand Magellan, who sailed for the king of Spain, led the first Spanish landing in the Philippines. He reached the island of Cebu in 1521.

In 1565, Miguel López de Legazpi founded a port on Cebu. It was the first permanent Spanish settlement. The Philippines is named for Philip II, who was king of Spain at that time. By the end of the 16ᵗʰ century, Spain controlled most of the Philippines. The Spanish were Roman Catholic. They convinced many local people to join their religion.

Many local tribal leaders helped the Spanish. However, Spain appointed its own government officials. The most important was the governor-general, who was also head of the church. The Spanish built churches, hospitals, and schools. They also introduced new ways of farming.

1564
Year that Miguel López de Legazpi, now buried in Manila, sailed from Mexico on his journey to the Philippines.

5 Number of ships Magellan led to the Philippines in 1521.

1571 Year that the capital city of Manila was founded.

Inside a chapel in Cebu City, wood encases the cross planted by Ferdinand Magellan on April 21, 1521. The painted ceiling shows his landing on the Philippine shore.

ROAD TO INDEPENDENCE

By the 17th century, many countries in Europe and Asia were buying agricultural products from the Philippines. Farms grew coffee, sugar, and **hemp**. The Spanish controlled most of this trade.

Many Filipinos grew unhappy under Spanish rule. In the 1870s, a group of educated Filipinos began a **movement** to change the way the Philippines was governed. They were led by José Rizal. The Spanish, fearful Rizal would start a revolution, arrested him in 1892. This led other activists to form a group called the Katipunan to fight for independence from Spain.

After being unfairly accused of violent activities, José Rizal was killed by the Spanish in 1896.

Revolution broke out in areas around Manila. Armed rebels fought against the Spanish army. An agreement ended the fighting in 1897, but rebel leaders continued to be discontent.

In April 1898, the Spanish-American War began between Spain and the United States. Filipino rebel leader Emilio Aguinaldo joined forces with the United States to defeat the Spanish in the Philippines. On June 12, 1898, Aguinaldo declared the Philippines independent from Spain.

The Battle of Manila Bay in 1898 was the first important U.S. victory in the Spanish-American War.

However, the peace treaty between the United States and Spain ending the Spanish-American War gave the United States control of the Philippines. It began to govern the area. Fighting broke out between Filipino and U.S. forces in 1899. It lasted for more than two years.

The United States said it would prepare the Philippines for future independence. It organized elections for local officials and helped form a Philippine legislature. In 1935, the Philippines became a self-governing U.S. commonwealth.

In December 1941, Japan invaded the Philippines during World War II. The United States regained control of the islands in 1944, and the next year, World War II ended with Japan's defeat. On July 4, 1946, the Philippines gained its independence from the United States.

Philippine forces fighting against U.S. control were weakened when their leader, Emilio Aguinaldo, was captured in 1901.

Road to Independence BY THE NUMBERS

1897
Year in which the flag of the Philippines was created.

$20 MILLION
Amount the United States paid Spain for the Philippines at the end of the Spanish-American War.

1992 Year the United States closed its last military base in the Philippines.

POPULATION

The Philippines has a population of more than 107 million people. That makes it the 12th most-populated nation in the world. Most of the residents live on only 11 islands. In fact, more than half of the country's residents live on the island of Luzon.

Almost half of Filipinos live in **urban** areas. The country's largest city is Quezon City, which is home to more than 2.6 million people. The next-largest city is Manila, with 1.6 million residents. The Manila area has a population of more than 12 million. Davao in Mindanao has more than 1.5 million residents.

A small number of **immigrants** live in the Philippines. Most have come from other countries in Asia. In recent years, many Filipinos have moved to other areas, often to seek better job opportunities. As of 2013, more than 10 million people born in the Philippines lived in other countries.

Population BY THE NUMBERS

ABout 2 Million
Number of people from the Philippines living in the United States.

72 Years
Life expectancy for people born in the Philippines.

3
Average number of children born to a Filipino family.

Open-air buses are often the fastest way for Filipinos to travel into the cities.

POLITICS AND GOVERNMENT

80 Number of provinces in the Philippines, each with its own local government.

15 Number of judges on the Supreme Court, the highest-level court in the Philippines.

1986 Year that Corazon Aquino was elected the first female president of the Philippines.

The Philippines has had periods of unrest since gaining independence. In 1972, President Ferdinand Marcos declared **martial law**. The government used force to stop protests, and it limited people's freedoms. Martial law was in effect until 1981. Then, in 1986, a movement began that forced Marcos from office and out of the country. A new **constitution** was created in 1987, and Filipinos have had greater freedom since that time.

The government of the Philippines is headed by the president. He or she is elected for a term of six years. A group of officials appointed by the president, called the cabinet, also helps run the country.

The Philippines has a Congress that passes the country's laws. Congress has two houses, or parts. They are the Senate, with 24 members, and the House of Representatives, with 287.

Every year, the Philippine president delivers a report on the state of the country to the Congress.

CULTURAL GROUPS

The largest cultural group in the Philippines is the Tagalog people. They traditionally live on Luzon. The Cebuano live on the Visayan islands. They make up one-fifth of the Philippine population. The Hiligayon people live on Panay and Negros. The Ilocano live in northern Luzon. The Bico are from Luzon's Bicol **Peninsula**. There are dozens of other cultural groups. When Chinese traders arrived in the 10th century, they became part of local culture. Many people in the country today have Chinese-Filipino ancestry.

Muslims on Mindanao sometimes perform dances in traditional costumes.

The main religion in the Philippines is Roman Catholicism. Islam is the second-largest religion. Many Muslims live on Mindanao. Some Muslim groups there have tried to separate from the Philippines and form their own country. There are also religions based on other cultural groups.

Basilica de Minore del Santo Niño in Cebu City, founded in 1565, is the oldest Roman Catholic Church in the Philippines.

The Philippines has two official languages. They are Filipino, based on the Tagalog language, and English. The United States began programs to teach English to Filipinos in the 1930s. By 1939, more Filipinos spoke English than any other language.

There are also eight major **dialects** in the Philippines. People on the island of Luzon speak Tagalog, Ilocano, and Bicol. Cebuano and Hiligaynon are spoken by residents of the Visayan islands. Other dialects include Waray, Pampango, and Pangasinan.

Many cultural groups have kept their history alive through the telling of stories. Some of the stories explain the beginning of the world. Others describe the origins of people. One epic story is called the *Darangen*. It tells a history of the Maranao people of Mindanao. The Ilocano people tell a legend of a traditional folk hero named Lamang.

About 88 percent of children ages 5 to 14 in the Philippines attend school.

ARTS AND ENTERTAINMENT

The University of Santo Tomas Museum is in Manila. Founded in the 17th century, it is the oldest museum in the Philippines. Its collections include artworks such as paintings and sculptures, as well as historical objects. The museum's natural history collection, which receives the most visitors, has exhibits about the animal and plant life of the Philippines.

José Rizal wrote the novel *Noli Me Tangere*, Latin for "Touch Me Not," in 1887.

Filipino authors have written popular and award-winning works in several languages. N. V. M. González, Nick Joaquin, Salvador Lopez, Benvenido Santos, and Linda Ty-Casper are examples of Filipino authors of English-language works. José Rizal, the independence leader, was also an author. His two novels were written in Spanish. The novels of Lualhati Bautista are in Tagalog.

Works of art are on display on the outside walls of San Agustin Church. It is the oldest church in Manila and dates back to 1607.

Many Filipino musicians have gained international recognition. Antonio J. Molina was an award-winning composer and conductor of classical music. He was named National Artist of the Philippines in 1973. Opera singer Jovita Fuentes made her stage debut in 1925 in Italy, a country known for its leading opera houses and performers. She won many international awards and founded the Artists Guild of the Philippines. This organization promotes opera in the country.

Lea Salonga, born in Manila in 1971, is an award-winning singer and actor. She has performed in musicals on Broadway and in London. She starred in the original stage production of *Miss Saigon* in 1989. Salonga also provided the singing voice for characters in the Disney animated films *Aladdin* and *Mulan*.

Apl.de.ap is an international Filipino pop music star. Born Allan Pineda Lindo in Pampanga, he is a founding member of the Black Eyed Peas. The group won three Grammy Awards in 2010, including Best Pop Vocal Album.

Arts and Entertainment BY THE NUMBERS

7 Lea Salonga's age when she first worked as a professional actor.

1973 Year the Philippines Philharmonic Orchestra was established.

About 75 Number of movies produced in the Philippines each year.

Apl.de.ap is a rapper, break dancer, and record producer.

SPORTS

Playing and watching sports is an important part of Filipino life. The Philippine Sports Commission, created in 1987, supports many sports programs. It also helps train athletes and develop their skills.

Lydia de Vega, who broke records in the 1980s, remains one of the Philippines' greatest track stars.

In 1924, the National Collegiate Athletic Association (NCAA) Philippines was created by Regino R. Ylanan, the head of physical education at the University of the Philippines. The association supports college athletes. Similar to the NCAA of the United States, the association sponsors several sports, including football, volleyball, and track and field. It has 10 member schools.

There are many amateur basketball teams throughout the country. The NCAA Philippines has held a basketball tournament since 1924. The Philippine Basketball Association is the world's second-oldest professional basketball league, after the National Basketball Association in the United States.

The national basketball team of the Philippines competes against other countries in tournaments such as the 2014 International Basketball Federation (FIBA) World Cup.

Boxers from the Philippines have won a number of international titles. Manny "Pacman" Pacquiao has won world titles in eight different weight classes since 1998. Three major boxing organizations named him the best fighter of the first decade of the 21st century. Since 2010, he has also been an elected member of the Philippines House of Representatives. In 2014, he became a player-coach for a Philippine Basketball Association team.

Track and field is another popular sport in the Philippines. Lydia de Vega held the record as the fastest woman in Asia from 1982 to 1990. The sprinter won nine gold medals and two silver medals in five South East Asia Games. She also won a gold medal at two Asian Games in a row.

Figure skater Michael Christian Martinez competed in the 2014 Winter Olympics in Sochi, Russia. He was the first Filipino figure skater ever to take part in the Olympics. He was also the first athlete in 22 years to compete for the Philippines in any sport at the Winter Games.

Manny Pacquiao has been called one of the best boxers in the world.

Sports BY THE NUMBERS

6 Number of gold medals basketball player Carlos Loyzaga, born in 1930, won at the Asian Games with his national team.

5 Number of times Jennifer Rosales of Manila won the Philippines Ladies Amateur Open, from 1994 to 1998.

17 Michael Christian Martinez's age when he competed in the 2014 Olympics.

Mapping the Philippines

We use many tools to interpret maps and to understand the locations of features such as cities, states, lakes, and rivers. The map below has many tools to help interpret information on the map of the Philippines.

Map of the Philippines

MAP LEGEND

★ Capital City
● City
🗺 Body of Water

〰 River
·-·-· Country Border
▲ Mountains

╲ Longitude & Latitude
▢ Philippines
▢ Other Countries

SCALE
0 — 150 Miles
0 — 150 Kilometers

N W E S

Mapping Tools

- The compass rose shows north, south, east, and west. The points in between represent northeast, northwest, southeast, and southwest.
- The map scale shows that the distant on a map represents much longer distance in real life. If you measure the distance between objects on a map, you can use the map scale to calculate the actual distance in miles or kilometers between those two points.

- The lines of latitude and longitude are long lines that appear on maps. The lines of latitude run east to west and measure how far north or south of the equator a place is located. The lines of longitude run north to south and measure how far east or west of the Prime Meridian a place is located. A location on a map can be found by using two numbers where latitude and longitude meet. This number is called a coordinate and is written using degrees and direction. For example, the city of Manila would be found at about 15°N and 121°E on a map.

Map It!

Using the map and the appropriate tools, complete the activities below.

Locating with latitude and longitude
1. Which city is located at 10°N and 124°E?
2. What peak is located at 7°N and 125°E?
3. Which city is located at 7°N and 126°E?

Distances between points
4. Using the map scale and a ruler, calculate the approximate distance between Manila and Baguio.
5. Using the map scale and a ruler, calculate the approximate distance between Baguio and Davao.
6. Using the map scale and a ruler, calculate the approximate distance between Cebu City and Quezon City.

ANSWERS 1. Cebu City 2. Mount Apo 3. Davao 4. 130 miles (200 km)
5. 700 miles (1000 km) 6. 350 miles (550 km)

Quiz Time

Test your knowledge of the Philippines by answering these questions.

1 What is the largest island in the Philippine archipelago?

2 What is the capital city of the Philippines?

3 Which mountain is the highest in the Philippines?

4 How much of the Philippines' electricity comes from hydropower?

5 In what year was Fort Santiago built?

6 What percentage of the labor force works in agriculture?

7 To which country does the Philippines export the most goods?

8 When did Spain establish the first permanent Spanish settlement in the Philippines?

9 On which date did the Philippines gain its independence from the United States?

10 What is the main religion of people in the Philippines?

ANSWERS

1. Luzon
2. Manila
3. Mount Apo, elevation 9,692 feet (2,954 m)
4. More than 20 percent
5. 1571
6. 32 percent
7. Japan
8. 1565
9. July 4, 1946
10. Roman Catholicism

Key Words

ancestors: people who lived in the past from whom a culture or person has descended

archipelago: a group of islands

architecture: the style in which buildings are designed

call centers: offices set up to handle a large number of business-related telephone calls

cassava: a tropical plant with a large root that is an important food source in many countries

colonial: relating to an area or country that is under the control of another country

commonwealth: an area that has some power to govern itself but that is under the authority of another country

constitution: a written document stating a country's basic principles and laws

dialects: forms of a language that are spoken or known only in certain areas or by certain groups of people

economy: the wealth and resources of a country or area

ethnic group: a group of people who share the same cultural background

fossil fuels: fuels such as coal, natural gas, and oil that formed from the remains of plants and animals that lived long ago

hemp: a plant from which rope, oil, and other goods are made

immigrants: people who move to a new country or area to live

labor force: the total number of workers in a country or area

life expectancy: the number of years that a person can expect to live

marine biologists: scientists who study life forms in the world's oceans and other saltwater environments

martial law: temporary military rule

monsoons: steady winds that bring moist air to a region at a certain time of year, causing long periods of heavy rain

movement: a series of organized activities to achieve a goal

peninsula: an area of land surrounded on three sides by water

planetarium: a museum with exhibits and shows about stars, planets, and other objects in space

renewable sources: sources of energy that will not run out for billions of years

republic: a type of government in which the people elect the country's head of state

reserves: the amount of oil available for future use

species: groups of individuals with common characteristics

trading partners: countries that a nation sells goods to and buys goods from

UNESCO: the United Nations Educational, Scientific, and Cultural Organization, whose main goals are to promote world peace and eliminate poverty through education, science, and culture

urban: relating to a city or town

Index

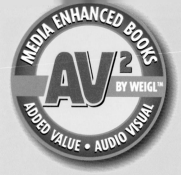

Log on to www.av2books.com

AV² by Weigl brings you media enhanced books that support active learning. Go to www.av2books.com, and enter the special code found on page 2 of this book. You will gain access to enriched and enhanced content that supplements and complements this book. Content includes video, audio, weblinks, quizzes, a slide show, and activities.

AV² Online Navigation

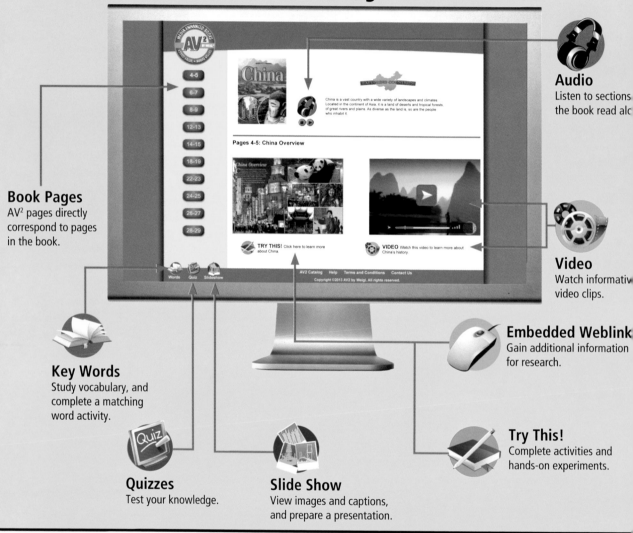

Audio
Listen to sections the book read alc

Book Pages
AV² pages directly correspond to pages in the book.

Video
Watch informativ video clips.

Key Words
Study vocabulary, and complete a matching word activity.

Embedded Weblink
Gain additional information for research.

Quizzes
Test your knowledge.

Slide Show
View images and captions, and prepare a presentation.

Try This!
Complete activities and hands-on experiments.

AV² was built to bridge the gap between print and digital. We encourage you to tell us what you like and what you want to see in the future.

Sign up to be an AV² Ambassador at www.av2books.com/ambassador.